Maggi and Milo

JULi BRENNiNG

· illustrated by ·

PRiSCiLLA BURRiS

SCHOLASTiC iNC.

To Coop and Doodle—
You can do it . . . whatever it is . . .
—J.B.

In memory of Casper Everest Burris,
our lovable and friendly dog.
—P.B.

ISBN 978-0-545-84928-9

Text copyright © 2014 by Juli Brenning. Pictures copyright © 2014 by Priscilla Burris.
All rights reserved. Published by Scholastic Inc., 557 Broadway, New York, NY 10012,
by arrangement with Dial Books for Young Readers, a division of Penguin Young Readers Group,
a member of Penguin Group (USA) LLC, A Penguin Random House Company.
SCHOLASTIC and associated logos are trademarks and/or registered trademarks of Scholastic Inc.

12 11 10 9 8 7 6 5 4 3 2 1   15 16 17 18 19 20/0

Printed in the U.S.A.   40

First Scholastic printing, January 2015

Designed by Jason Henry
Text set in Rough LT Com
The artwork for this book was created digitally.

This is Maggi.

Maggi is an excellent adventurer, a pretty good songwriter, a bit of a scientist, and Milo's very best friend.

This is Milo.

Milo is a dog.

And this is the awesome package Maggi's grandma sent.

It had all the necessities for a frog hunt—boots
and knowledge.

(Country dogs, like Milo, don't wear boots.)

That night Maggi told Milo, "We need to get a good night's sleep. Tomorrow we hunt frogs!"

The next morning, Maggi pulled on her new blue boots, which were perfect for this kind of adventure, and her favorite dress, which was just plain perfect.

Well . . . almost.
Maggi ran back
to the bathroom to
brush her teeth which
she had *completely*
forgotten to do.

At breakfast, Maggi handed a note to her brother that said:

PLEASE KEEP THE CHITCHAT TO A MINIMUM. I'M IN A HURRY!

Her brother rolled his eyes, which is apparently how twelve-year-olds communicate.

Maggi focused. Eating quickly requires serious concentration. Breakfast took exactly 11 ¾ bites. . . .

Then she was off . . . for real this time.

"I am FROG HUNTER!"

shouted Maggi.

Stopping at the edge of the world,
she called,

"Milo!"

"I am FROG HUNTER...
and he is Milo!"

Together, Maggi and Milo
ran down the hill,

past the chicken coop,

through the valley of the ferns,

and all the way
to the pond, where . . .

Maggi tested the waterproofness of her new blue boots.

After sufficient stomping, she announced, "Milo, my feet are *perfectly* dry." That's important.

"Grandma always says, 'wet feet make for a very long day.'"

(Which is true, wet feet *do* make for a long day.)

Maggi stood in the water.
She waited for a frog.

Maggi waited
a million minutes.
Nothing happened.

This was BORING. Boring in all capital letters, BORING!

Maggi sang a song.
She sang about frogs and waiting and blue boots.

Milo wandered off.

So far, this was not working out as planned.

"Milo!" called Maggi.
He wasn't there.

"MmmMiiiiiiiil1l0!"

Maggi tried very hard *not* to think about losing Milo or being alone.

In front of her, the cattails moved.
"Milo? Is that you?" she asked, *trying* to sound brave.
Slowly, Maggi pulled apart the cattails . . .

and there in the muck was Milo!

And a frog!

Milo had found a FROG!

Maggi reached down and caught that frog.

"Hi. I'm Maggi and this is Milo. You will be called Alexander. *Welcome* to our pond."

Gently, Maggi placed Alexander back into the water.
She had to be very careful, frogs are *terribly* squirmy.

"Milo you are SO smart!" squealed Maggi.

(This is a true statement; border collies are *very* smart.)

Milo barked, wagged his tail, and ran to another spot. Maggi followed close behind. And there in the muck was another frog!

Maggi named the second frog Benjamin, the third one Cooper,
the fourth one Daniel . . .

(See the pattern?)

After meeting Oliver, Maggi realized all the frogs they had found were boys!

That was ABSURD!

"The world does not need any more boys!" Maggi proclaimed.

She found Princess Penelope under a lily pad.

Holding her newest catch, Maggi said, "Milo, there is NO WAY I can think of a girl's name that begins with the letter Q."

So Maggi and Milo rested.

(It's not easy work, this frog hunting.)

As Milo slept, Maggi sang a song. A quiet,
end-of-the-day kind of song.

Afterward, Maggi and Milo walked home,

through the valley of the ferns,

past the chicken coop,

and all the way back up the hill.

Just as the sun was setting, they heard
the most marvelous music.

Side by side, they sat on the edge of the world,
just listening to the frogs say good night.

When the last note faded,
Maggi said,

"Milo, that was
the very best day!
I cannot wait for our
next adventure!"